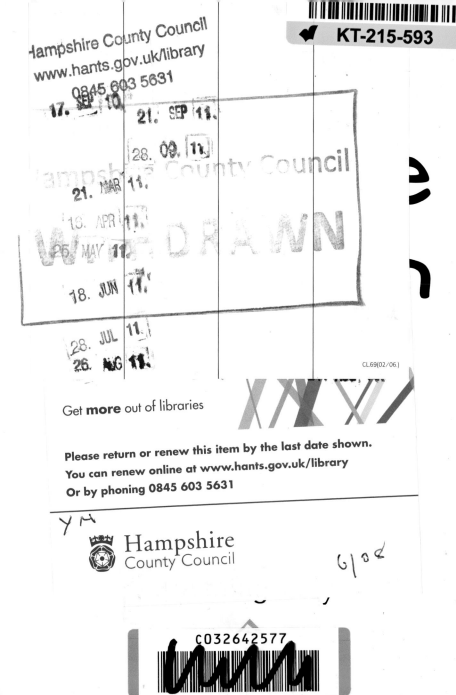

First published in 2007 by
Franklin Watts
338 Euston Road
London
NW1 3BH

Franklin Watts Australia
Level 17 / 207 Kent Street
Sydney
NSW 2000

A CIP catalogue record for this book is available
from the British Library.

ISBN 978 0 7496 7141 9 (hbk)
ISBN 978 0 7496 7700 8 (pbk)

Series Editor: Jackie Hamley
Series Advisors: Dr Barrie Wade, Dr Hilary Minns
Series Designer: Peter Scoulding

Printed in China

Franklin Watts is a division of
Hachette Children's Books,
an Hachette Livre UK company.

READING CORNER

Georgie
and the Dragon
the

Written by
Sue Graves

Illustrated by
François Hall

W
FRANKLIN WATTS
LONDON•SYDNEY

Sue Graves

"I would love to go to knight school like Georgie. It would be fun to learn how to scare away dragons ... so long as they weren't too big!"

François Hall

"I once had to get rid of a big scary monster – by showing it my drawing of an even bigger and scarier monster. I'm pleased to say it hasn't been seen since."

Georgie went to Knight School.

She went there every day.

She had to learn
a lot of things,

Dragon
scaring

like scaring dragons away.

One day, an enormous
dragon came.

His name was Smokey Joe.

The knights tried hard
to frighten him.

But Joe just wouldn't go!

"I've got a plan," said Georgie.
"I'll make that dragon shake.

13

She picked up an old bucket
and went down to the lake.

"I've got a surprise for you!"
said Georgie to Smokey Joe.

16

Joe looked in the bucket ...

Then you should have
seen him go!

23

Notes for parents and teachers

READING CORNER has been structured to provide maximum support for new readers. The stories may be used by adults for sharing with young children. Primarily, however, the stories are designed for newly independent readers, whether they are reading these books in bed at night, or in the reading corner at school or in the library.

Starting to read alone can be a daunting prospect. **READING CORNER** helps by providing visual support and repeating words and phrases, while making reading enjoyable. These books will develop confidence in the new reader, and encourage a love of reading that will last a lifetime!

If you are reading this book with a child, here are a few tips:

1. Talk about the story before you start reading. Look at the cover and the title. What might the story be about? Why might the child like it?

2. Encourage the child to reread the story, and to retell the story in their own words, using the illustrations to remind them what has happened.

3. Discuss the story and see if the child can relate it to their own experience, or perhaps compare it to another story they know.

4. Give praise! Small mistakes need not always be corrected.

READING CORNER covers three grades of early reading ability, with three levels at each grade. Each level has a certain number of words per story, indicated by the number of bars on the spine of the book, to allow you to choose the right book for a young reader:

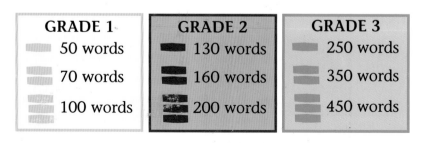

GRADE 1	GRADE 2	GRADE 3
50 words	130 words	250 words
70 words	160 words	350 words
100 words	200 words	450 words